I See the Moon
and the Moon Sees Me

By Jonathan London
Illustrated by Peter Fiore

PUFFIN BOOKS

I see the moon
and the moon sees me.
God bless the moon,
and God bless me.
　　　　—Traditional

I see the sun
and the sun sees me.
Hello sun,
how do you be?

I see the sea
and the sea sees me.
Hello sea,
are you shining for me?

I see the river
and the river sees me.
Hello river,
are you talking to me?

I see the mountains
and the mountains see me.
Hello mountains,
will you echo for me?

I see the tree
and the tree sees me.
Hello tree,
are you waving at me?

I see the birds
and the birds see me.
Hello birds,
are you singing to me?

I see the flowers
and the flowers see me.
Hello flowers,
are you smiling for me?

I see the bee
and the bee sees me.
Hello bee,
are you buzzing for me?

I see the bee
and it's following me.
Goodbye bee—
Oops! Now there are three!

I see the lake
and the lake sees me.
Hello lake,
now I am free.

I see a star
and the star sees me.
Hello star,
are you winking at me?

I see my house
and my house sees me.
Hello house,
were you waiting for me?

I see the moon
and the moon sees me.
Hello moon . . .

. . . will you dream with me?

For the little ones
—J. L.

For my Megan
—P. F.

PUFFIN BOOKS
Published by the Penguin Group
Penguin Putnam Inc., 375 Hudson Street, New York, New York 10014, U.S.A.
Penguin Books Ltd, 27 Wrights Lane, London W8 5TZ, England
Penguin Books Australia Ltd, Ringwood, Victoria, Australia
Penguin Books Canada Ltd, 10 Alcorn Avenue, Toronto, Ontario, Canada M4V 3B2
Penguin Books (N.Z.) Ltd, 182-190 Wairau Road, Auckland 10, New Zealand

Penguin Books Ltd, Registered Offices: Harmondsworth, Middlesex, England

First published in the United States of America by Viking,
a division of Penguin Books USA Inc., 1996
Published in Puffin Books, 1998

3 5 7 9 10 8 6 4 2

Text copyright © Jonathan London, 1996
Illustrations copyright © Peter Fiore, 1996
All rights reserved

THE LIBRARY OF CONGRESS HAS CATALOGED THE VIKING EDITION AS FOLLOWS:
London, Jonathan. I see the moon and the moon sees me /
[adapted and expanded] by Jonathan London;
illustrated by Peter Fiore. p. cm.
Summary: An expansion of the classic nursery rhyme into a text which captures a child's
perfect day in the midst of mountains, trees, flowers, and other aspects of nature.
ISBN 0-670-85918-4
1. Children's poetry, American. 2. Nature—Juvenile poetry.
[1. American poetry. 2. Nursery rhymes.] I. Fiore, Peter M., ill. II. Title.
PS3562.04874I48 1996 811'.54—dc20 95-34558 CIP AC

Puffin Books ISBN 0-14-055487-4

Printed in the United States of America